W9-BQW-003

Loud

Soft

Jiggly

Boinging

In a tunnel

Through a funnel

Wobbly

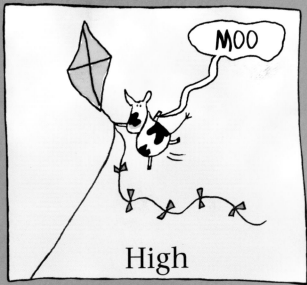

High

Low

Moo–sical

Smooth

Sleeping

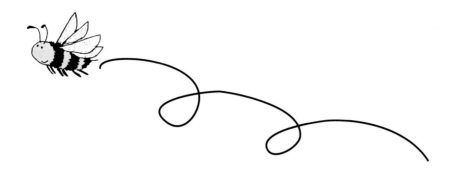

To all the cows.
And a big Mooo to Lina, Joe, Renate, Saul, David,
Rachel, Heather, Elaine, Caroline and Eliz.

First edition for the United States and Canada published in 2002 by
Barron's Educational Series, Inc.

© Deborah Fajerman 2002

The right of Deborah Fajerman
to be identified as the author and illustrator of this work has been asserted in
accordance with the Copyrights, Designs and Patents Act 1988

First published in the United Kingdom in 2002 by
RANDOM HOUSE CHILDREN'S BOOKS
61-63 Uxbridge Rd, London W5 5SA
A division of The Random House Group Ltd

All inquiries should be addressed to:
Barron's Educational Series, Inc.
250 Wireless Boulevard
Hauppauge, NY 11788
http://www.barronseduc.com

Library of Congress Catalog Card Number 2002101205

International Standard Book Number 0-7641-2285-1

Printed in Singapore
9 8 7 6 5 4 3 2 1

How to Speak

MOO!

Deborah Fajerman

BARRON'S

The cow language is called Moo
and every single word is moo.

So, you think that all moos sound the same?
Well, think again.

Moo can be so loud
it is heard from miles around.

And Moo can be so soft
you hardly hear a sound.

Moo depends a lot on size.
Big cows do lows,
little ones, highs.

MOO

When cows jump on a trampoline
their moos go up and down.

And when they go to sleep
their moos lie on the ground.

Every day at TV time
the cows are always mellow.

But "Moo" sounds very wobbly
when they jiggle on some Jell-O.

Cows never moo when they eat their lunch. The sound they make is munch munch munch munch.

Moo sounds funny through a funnel

and even stranger in a tunnel.

A cow in a rowboat gently glides along
which makes its moo sound as sweet as a song

Cow on skateboard – path is lumpy.

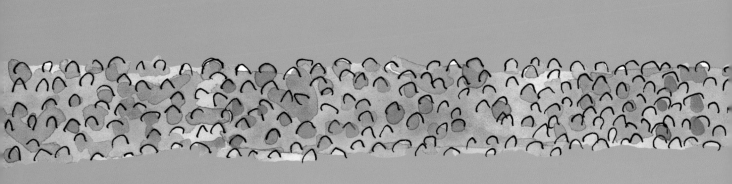

Cow is jiggly – moo is jumpy.

The language cows know best is Moo.
But they know some other words too.

High moo, low moo, soft moo, loud moo,
All-together moos make the very best...

m m m m m m . . .

Loud

Soft

Jiggly

Boinging

In a tunnel

Through a funnel

Wobbly

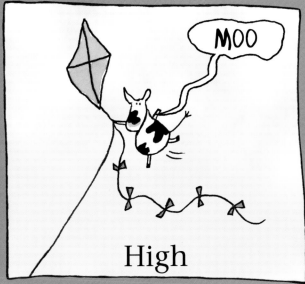

High

Low

Moo–sical

Smooth

Sleeping